Shattered HOME

A Coming Home Series Novella

J.M. ADELE

SHATTERED HOME
© J.M. Adele, 2017.
All Rights Reserved

Edited by Eeva Lancaster
Cover Design by Book Flare Publishers
Cover Photo from Adobe Stock © e_serebryakova
Formatted by Book Flare Publishers

Print Edition
ISBN: 978-0-9944516-7-5

Dedicated to any child who has ever felt unloved.
The truth is you are lovable.
Believe that and you will be free.

Contents

Chapter One

Aiden kicked at the dirt with the toe of his shoe, watching the dust curl up to his knees before it settled back down. He stood at the edge of the school yard, listening to all the kids squeal and yell in delight at their game of tag. They all seemed to know each other, calling out each other's names. He recognized a few faces as they shot past, but he'd never spent much time outside of his yard to meet the other kids.

Aiden shuffled his weight to ease the pain in his behind. After a whupping last night, he'd spent four hours locked in his room before his father made him scrub the kitchen floor. It was his own fault. He knew he shouldn't have peed in the garden. He hadn't wanted to go back in the house, and didn't think his father would be watching. Now, he knew. His father always had his eyes on him.

Again, he kicked the dirt, shoulders sagging because he was too tired to join in the fun. It wasn't exactly the first day of school he'd imagined, but he was still happy to be there. He was happy to be anywhere, but home.

A girl with black pigtails flashed by, four kids trailing her as she cackled. With a burst of speed, she left them behind and disappeared. Aiden stood up straight, craning his neck to get a better view.

Where'd she go?

He thought he'd seen her before, or maybe a girl with the same hair, swinging on the tire swing in front of the big white house down the road from home. He dreamed about that house. Playing out all sorts of adventures where he got to be the hero, the knight, the soldier, the king … His imagination was endless. Sometimes, he would dream about a little girl with black hair. Swinging on that tire, she looked like an angel to him, kicking her legs out with her hair flowing behind.

The children all scattered; some starting a game of catch, some climbing on the jungle gym. He took a couple of steps closer, but couldn't see her anywhere. Maybe it wasn't the same girl.

Feeling a light tap on his shoulder, Aiden jerked and spun around.

"Hi."

His jaw fell slack. There she was. Waving at him, and smiling a gap-toothed smile. He squinted down at her, almost needing to shield his eyes from the sun reflecting off her pale skin. She looked like she was glowing, and her green eyes twinkled in the light. Like the grass after the rain had given it a drink. Maybe she really was an angel.

"Can't you speak? 'Cause if you can't speak, we could write to each other instead. Can you write? My daddy taught me how to write my name, and the alphabet. I know how to count to twenty-seven." Poking a thumb at her chest, she beamed with pride.

Aiden blinked and took a step back.

"Don't be scared. I just wanted to ask if you wanna play. You should join in. Everybody here's friendly."

He swallowed, and scrubbed his knuckles over his eyes to check that they were working. "Are you an angel?"

She bobbed her head. "Yeah. How'd ya know?"

A swarm of bees burst into his tummy. *She's a real angel.*

"You look like one." He rubbed his palms on his thighs, and swiped the back of his hand under his nose.

Her dark brows dipped low. "What's an angel s'posed to look like?"

"Pretty and glowing, and stuff." He shrugged his stiff shoulders, rubbing his sweaty hands again.

Her mouth pouted before tipping up into a beaming grin. "Well, thank you. My mama always told me to say thank you when someone says something nice about me. She's gone to heaven. Daddy said they needed more angels, so she had to go. I hope they don't need me 'cause I don't want to leave my daddy alone." She waved a finger at his head. "You have nice hair. It's the same color as the sand at the beach. Have you ever been to the beach?"

Aiden's head reeled, trying to keep up. "No." His shoulders slumped and he picked at a loose thread on his shirt.

"Ooh, it's so much fun." She clasped her hands in front of her chest. "I'll ask my daddy if you can come with us when we go next time. We always go with my uncles and aunts, and my cousins. We'll teach you how to build a sand castle."

"Okay."

He folded his arms behind his back, crossing his fingers that Sir would let him go. He'd seen the beach on TV. It did look fun. But what had the nerves buzzing in his belly was the thought of spending time with a real angel. She made him feel all tingly inside. He liked it.

"I hope they don't need you back in heaven, either." He sent her a shy smile.

"I'll just tell them I can't go." She shrugged and propped her hands on her hips. "What's your name?"

"Aiden Thomas."

"Are you a fast runner?"

"I think so."

Maybe not after his punishment last night. He could be, though. He'd try to be, for her.

Slapping a hand on his arm, she yelled, "Tag! You're it," before dashing off, leaving him in another cloud of dust.

The farther away she got, the harder the tug on his chest, like she had tied him with a rope. It took his feet a while to get moving. He wondered if he was having another one of his dreams as he watched her run, eyeing him over her shoulder. There was no way he was pinching himself out of this one. He'd never felt more awake.

He'd found a real live angel. Aiden's prayers had been answered.

———

Almost Eleven Years Later

"Mornin', Daddy. How'd you sleep?"

Angel scraped the wooden spoon through the eggs to scramble them a bit more, before scooping a serving onto a plate for her pa.

He shuffled into the kitchen, his black hair flat on one side and standing up on the other. Speaking through a yawn, his answer was almost indecipherable, "Still 'sleep."

"Why don't you go in late this mornin'? I'm sure Harry and Harvey have things under control."

He dragged a hand down his face and scrubbed it through his beard, tired blue eyes struggling to focus on her. "I can't. I have a meeting with the architect about the expansion. We all have to be there."

He took a seat and she pushed the plate under his nose, handing him some silverware. "You're workin' too hard. What time did you get home last night?"

His gaze slid to the clock. "Five hours ago."

Her tongue clicked against the roof of her mouth, as she made a plate for herself and joined him at the breakfast bar. Spearing some eggs, she held back from telling him off. He was still half asleep, and it wasn't her place to be telling her daddy anything, anyways. Not that it had stopped her before. She just tried to be subtle about it. They were a team. They had to look after each other. She glided the salt shaker across the countertop as a peace offering.

"You're so much like her, ye know." Her daddy fixed his eyes on her forehead, seeing through her to some other time. "Your mama, she'd scold me for losing track of time and working into the early hours. Then she'd look after me, and I'd kick my own tail for missing out on precious moments with her. I still do."

"Aw, Daddy, don't do that. Mama loved that you worked hard to achieve your dreams. When I had nightmares, she used to say to me that I could chase the bad dreams away by thinking of bigger and better things. She said that my daddy was the biggest dreamer of all, and that I had the ability to dream big and be just like you. Because I was a Murphy, too. I thought it was your super power for a while." Blinking away the sting of tears, she laughed.

Lines etched deep into his temples as he smiled at the memory. "She always made me feel like I was her hero. The truth is, she was mine. I hope you have the same someday. Your partner should be someone who builds you up and makes you want to be the best you can be." Blue eyes twinkled as they assessed her. "I suspect he's not too far away."

She returned her daddy's perusal, a twinkle of her own probably reflecting back.

He wasn't too far at all.

Just down the road, in fact.

———

Angel straddled the sturdy sycamore branch, pretending to concentrate on her loose shoe laces as she swung her legs. Fleeting glimpses at her golden-haired companion betrayed the true recipient of her focus. Out of the corner of her eye, she watched as he ripped long blades of grass into thin strips and sent them twirling to the ground. Each piece of green debris mimicked the fluttering behind her breast bone, induced by being so close to him.

She leaned forward, the tender skin of her palms scratched by the rough bark, and contemplated lacing her shoes. Anything to keep her mind from fixating on Aiden's hands, and what else he could be doing with them. She wasn't sure she was even ready to be having such thoughts. Angel sighed. She was only sixteen, for Lord's sake. Her mother was probably turning over in her grave.

She looked towards the house, knowing that she wouldn't be able to see the old, southern colonial house from this far back in the yard, but still double checking that they were a safe distance away from the prying eyes of her father.

Once again, her eyes flicked back to their target, heat suffusing her cheeks when she locked onto his whiskey-toned gaze. He smirked and threw a blade of grass into her lap.

"What's goin' on in that head of yours?" Aiden's teenage vocal chords hadn't yet settled on a comfortable pitch, making Angel giggle as the words squeaked and dipped their way out.

"Oh, just enjoying the warm breeze." *And watching you, thinking of our first kiss.*

The wind picked up her hair, blowing it across her face. She pulled it back, inspecting its bottle-red color, glad that her black regrowth was hidden under her hat. Twirling a strand around her thumb, she brushed the ends along the crease of her lips, enjoying the pleasant tingle. It wasn't as good as having his lips on hers, though. It'd been over a week since he'd kissed her, but she still remembered the soft feel of his flesh pressing against hers. When the heck he'd pluck up the courage to do it again, she didn't know. But she was too chicken to take matters into her own hands. It was supposed to be up to the boy to make the moves.

She shoved the air out of her lungs in frustration, at the same time she heard his breath stutter. Catching him fixated on what she was doing with her hair, she dropped the strands, sat up straight, pushed up her glasses, and crossed her ankles. Maybe she *was* chicken, but he was probably feeling the same thing. This was Alabama. Southern girls were supposed to be strong. There was nothing wrong with taking charge occasionally. Was there? Besides, if she didn't do something soon, she'd die of yearning.

"Are you ever gonna kiss me again?" She swallowed against a dry mouth, and ordered her galloping heart to settle down.

"Hell, yes."

A buzzing in her belly joined the galloping, and her confidence swelled. *That was a yes*. His gaze was still attached to her mouth, but he wasn't moving his lips any closer.

She tutted at his language and his lack of action, raising her eyebrows. "When?"

"I've been waiting for the right moment." He licked his lips and raised his eyes to hers.

"Well, now's good …" She leaned forward putting her face directly in front of his. "… in case you were wondering."

His warm palms landed on her cheeks and he slammed his mouth on hers, pushing her off balance, and nearly dislodging her from the tree. Letting out a squeak of surprise, she slapped her hands down on his thighs to stop from falling, and felt something hard under her grip. Aiden reared back, spitting out a frenzy of curses, putting her off balance again.

Angel blinked back hot tears at his rejection. It wasn't until his hands clasped at his crotch, his body recoiling against the trunk, and far away from her, that she clued in to what she'd done.

Her eyelids levered wide. "Oh, Lord. I'm so sorry."

Scooting her tail backwards, she locked her ankles together to secure her perch, and covered her mouth with both hands. If she was ever going to use a swear word, now would be the time. But, she pushed her fingers firmly into her cheeks, until her teeth started to ache.

Aiden's face was set in a grimace, but he let out a pained laugh. He couldn't seriously think this was funny. She loosened her hands and watched as his smile grew more genuine, his body unfurling from the fetal position. He was lucky he'd been leaning against the trunk, or he'd have been on the grass with something else broken besides his ... boy bits.

The corners of her lips tipped up, a snort escaping. She blushed, slapping a hand back over her mouth. Not only because snorting was unladylike, but because she didn't mean to laugh at his predicament.

Aiden had no qualms about vocalizing his amusement. He tipped his head back, opened his mouth wide, and let out his raucous laughter. She had no choice but to join him, dissolving into a fit of giggles. It was such a rare thing to hear him laugh like that. Angel sincerely hoped she didn't have to punch him in the ... boy bits ... to hear it again.

"Shit, that hurt."

"Aiden! Language."

"Sorry, but it did."

"Yeah, I noticed. I am sorry. I didn't mean to ... you know." She looked at his lap briefly, before inspecting her shoe laces again. "I wasn't expecting it."

"It?"

"Don't make me say the words."

"My erection?"

She gasped and chewed on her lips, watching a smirk play on his face.

"I can't help it. It happens a lot when I'm alone with you."

The buzzing in her belly turned to a roar, sending a power surge through her body with its force. "Oh, my God. Would you please stop?"

Her words were bashful, but she was proud of herself for having that effect on him. She wasn't completely naive. She'd pinched one of her aunt's romance novels and hidden it under her mattress for weeks, soaking up the newfound knowledge any chance she got. Luckily, she'd been making her own bed for a while now, and didn't have to worry about her daddy discovering her secret.

She straightened up and smiled. "Could we try that again?"

"Hell, yeah." Angel smacked a hand on his chest as he lurched forward.

"Language!"

"Sorry." His face scrunched before relaxing into a wry smile. "How about I pay for my sins with a kiss?"

She narrowed her eyes, but couldn't stop the grin. "Yeah, okay."

This time he let her move toward him slowly, putting his hands on her waist to steady her. The gentle

J.M. ADELE

touch burned through her T-shirt. His fingers flexed and pressed into her flesh like he wanted to hold her tighter, or maybe remove the pesky fabric between them. She had no doubt they'd get to that point eventually, but not while they were perched in their tree, with her father not that far away.

Placing her hands on his shoulders, she reveled in their hasty rise and fall, knowing that she was near to panting with excitement herself. This boy was hers. He always will be. She just knew it. When his lips met hers again, all her nerve endings came alive, flushing her body with a euphoria only he could instill. The sound of their mingled breaths joined the smacking of lips, driving her excitement higher. She instinctively moved closer, climbing into his lap, and wrapping her legs over his. She wasn't worried about falling, she knew he wouldn't let her.

Aiden pulled back, resting his head on the tree, and gave her a satisfied grin that mirrored her own. "I wish I had my camera right now. I want to capture the look on your face."

"You take too many photos already."

She slid her arms closer and locked her hands behind his neck, ready for another drugging kiss. Maybe she'd try tongue this time.

"Aiden?"

Angel twisted her head at the sound of her pa's booming voice coming from a distance.

"Shit!" Aiden pushed on her waist in a panic.

She had to laugh as she moved back to a safe distance. "I'll let you have that one for free."

His face drained of color, and his throat moved like he was trying to swallow a melon. Her daddy loved Aiden, since the first time she brought him home after preschool. She couldn't see the threat of a shotgun any time soon, but now that they were more than friends, maybe her father wouldn't deal so well with his little girl growing up.

She saw her pa's wavy, black hair appear above the bushes, before his mammoth, muscled frame stepped into the clearing under the tree.

"There y'are." He shoved his motor-oil-smeared hands in his pockets and narrowed his eyes, considering them for a moment.

She gripped the branch a little tighter, suddenly worried that the threat of his shotgun might not be so ridiculous after all.

"Aiden. Your father is looking for ye. You'd better go on home, it's supper time. Come in and get washed up."

"Is he here?"

Aiden's voice broke on the words, but she knew it wasn't his immature vocal cords causing the problem. Aiden might have feared her pa, but she'd never seen anything put more fear in him than his own father.

Mr. Thomas ran a law practice in town, and had a reputation for being a wolf with sharp fangs. She suspected he was just as awful at home as he was in the courtroom, but she'd never been inside Aiden's house to see for herself.

"No. He demanded to be let in, but I sent him away."

Angel scrambled down the tree after Aiden, landing behind where he stood before her father. He tugged at his clothes, looking like he'd rather do anything else besides go home.

Her daddy laid his large hand on Aiden's shoulder, squeezing in a silent show of support before leading him off. She trailed behind them through the thick undergrowth, raising her feet high with each step, and thinking how blessed she was to have her daddy. He knew when a person needed comfort, and he'd always been generous in giving it. He probably knew exactly what was going on in the house down the street, but he'd never discuss it with her. If there was one thing wrong between her and Aiden, it was her exclusion from his family life. She'd guessed why, but it still didn't sit well with her. He always shut her out. He should've known better. It just made her want to fight harder. If she had to march down the road and bang down his door to finally gain entry, she'd do it. The time was coming. Her patience was threatening to snap.

Chapter Two

Aiden dumped his bike around the side of his house and ran up the back steps, entering through the kitchen door. His mother sat at the table, ignoring her plate of roast vegetables and chicken, preferring to cradle her glass of red wine. She didn't bother with a greeting, and he didn't expect one. It was their routine. She only acknowledged him in public.

Her disregard wasn't what made his stomach drop to his toes. It was the gravy smeared plate stacked next to the sink. It was the newspaper spread open to hide all but his father's clenched hands, and the slicked back, blonde hair on top of his head. It was the thunder clouds gathering behind his father's eyes as the paper lowered, and Sir stood to his full height.

He was late for dinner.

He was so dead.

Aiden struggled to keep his body from shaking. His palm, slick with sweat, slipped on the door knob as he closed the door behind him.

He watched in resignation, fighting back tears, as his father started to unbuckle his belt.

"I'm going to assume that since you weren't home in time for dinner, you mustn't be hungry."

The smell of the roast meal lingered deliciously in the air. He was hungry. But not starving, thanks to an extra slice of Angel's chocolate cake that afternoon.

"I'm sorry I'm late, Sir."

"Did I say you could speak, boy?" Spit flew from his father's mouth, landing on the table.

Aiden pressed his lips together, and watched his mother vacate the room, like she always did when this happened. More tears threatened. His stupid tear ducts needed to grow up. He wasn't five anymore. He should be used to the sting of betrayal and abandonment by now.

"Take off your shirt and drop your pants."

He did as he was told, fumbling, and silently cursing his trembling hands. His father moved behind him, pushing him towards the table and shoving his back, so he had no choice but to lean down and hang on.

"You've been over at the Murphy's again. I know that's where you go. Hank can deny it all he likes. That bastard and his spawn have been filling your head with all sorts of fairytales about how life should be. What's the matter, boy, your family not good enough for you?"

Aiden jerked, pulling in a shaky breath as the first blow landed across the middle of his back.

"Those grease monkeys aren't fit to mix with my blood." Sir leaned over Aiden, growling directly into his ear. "Why would they want an outsider tagging along, getting in their way? You're not one of them. You never will be."

The lash of the belt struck Aiden with enough force to make his eyes roll back in his head. He clenched his teeth harder, and dug his fingers into the edge of the table, jerking with each blow.

"You got your eye on Murphy's daughter? She's only useful for spreading her legs, but you won't be mixing our blood and tying us to that family for good. I won't have it."

The vitriol spewed from his father's mouth, thick as molasses. Aiden felt it clogging his lungs and pounding his ears, dragging him under its hatred, and feeding his own hatred for this man. He wanted to fight back, to defend the girl he loved. How dare Sir speak about her like that. She was everything that was good and pure in his world.

The next three lashes struck in quick succession, making him throw his head back at the searing pain cutting deeper each time. He wondered how many his father would be giving him, and how many more years he would have to endure this torture. If it wasn't for the Murphys, he'd have run already.

"The Thomas name is something to be respected and upheld. Until you get that through your head, I forbid you to leave this house."

Aiden's body was wrenched upright, his upper arm caught in a bear-trap hold as his father heaved his limp body up the stairs to his bedroom. Thrown face first onto the bed, he lay still, listening to the click of the lock sealing his cell. Raw nerve endings screamed in agony across his back and the top of his ass, and his lungs struggled for air. He tried to stop the freight train of loathing that was gathering momentum. Aimed mostly at himself, because despite his parents' mistreatment of him … he still loved them, and wanted desperately to please. And, didn't that make him a dumb fuck.

Groaning, he rolled his head to the side, and folded his hands under his cheek for a pillow. The stupid tears he'd been fighting oozed onto his hands, and his nose leaked all over the bed in a trail of mucus. He couldn't be bothered wiping the mess away. He knew his pain wasn't done. Not even close. He'd wear it like a tattoo for a while yet.

Closing his eyes, he willed all the bad shit away, replacing it with images of Angel sitting in that tree. Her floppy hat and baggy T-shirt. The laces of her shoes dangling in the breeze, and the reflection of light filtered through the canopy on her glasses. Her coy smile. Her huge green eyes.

His teeth hurt from grinding them so hard, but a smile still hinted despite the pain. Angel had asked him to kiss her. She'd been eager enough to risk falling out of the tree by climbing into his lap, and aligning him with the gates of heaven.

Her parents had been insightful when they'd named her. She was an angel. His Angel. If he could be a part of her life forever, he'd be the luckiest son of a bitch. Aiden worried that her association with him was dragging her name through the filth, not the other way around.

Pfft. His father didn't know shit.

He groaned and threw a hand over his face to block the morning sun filtering through his eyelids, hissing at the pain the movement caused. Rubbing the grit away from his eyes with his thumb, he attempted to pry them open and get his bearings. As if the pain in his back wasn't enough of a reminder, his ready-to-burst bladder, and dry-as-a-dessert mouth, did a great job at slapping him back to reality. He needed to find a pot plant, or something. Fast.

Spying his baseball bag, he prayed to God that he'd forgotten to take out his water bottle as he hobbled over. The zip parted to reveal his plastic savior, half full, even. He raised his eyes to the ceiling muttering, "Amen."

Downing the liquid in two huge gulps, he then used the bottle to relieve himself. *Desperate times and all that.* He'd need to prepare an emergency stash of food, water, and a piss container for the future.

The thought had him wondering how in hell he'd ended up in this situation. His friends didn't have to worry about their basic human needs being met, for Christ's sake.

He hid the bottle under his bed, noticing several smears of blood on the sheets. *Sonofabitch, he made me bleed.*

The click of the lock releasing had his head snapping up, and sent his heart thundering in preparation for another fight.

Sir poked his head around the door. "Clean yourself up and get to school."

He was gone before Aiden could reply. Not that he had anything to say to the man. Except maybe, *why? Why are you such a bastard? Why don't you love me?*

The ground swayed under his feet, and he lowered his butt to the bed. How the hell was he supposed to go to school? He'd probably feel better after some food and pain killers, but even then, every move made him relive yesterday's horror. His brain began to float between his ears, and the room appeared to warp out of shape. Flopping to the side, he hoped his head would hit somewhere close to the pillow, as he cried out in agony.

Aiden kept his eyes closed, pulling in air through flared nostrils, until the room stopped imitating a Tilt-A-Whirl. He knew his father would be back to check on him. He had to think of a plan to get out before then. If he could get himself dressed and down the stairs, he might be able to make it to Angel's house. But, he didn't want her to see him like this. Shit, no, that was no good. If he could get dressed and get to a phone, he could ring Hank at the garage. He was the only one Aiden could trust to help him without saying anything to anyone.

He gripped the edge of his mattress in one hand and lowered a foot to the floor, sliding the rest of his body down to follow. Crawling on hands and knees, he made it to his dresser without the room spinning, but couldn't stop the whimpers of pain. He'd been beaten up plenty of times before, but not like this. His father's rage was growing, and Aiden was the outlet.

After an awkward struggle, he managed to get dressed, and shuffled on his tail down the stairs to the living room where the phone was. The only sounds in the house were his labored breaths and the dial tone as he picked up the receiver, punching in the number of the garage.

"Harvey's Auto Shop. If it's broke, we'll fix it. How can we help you today?" Damn, it was Tina, the office manager.

He hoped she didn't recognize his voice. He hoped his voice didn't desert him.

"Uh, hi. I'd like to speak to Hank, if he's there, please."

"Sure thing, honey. Hold on a sec."

The hold music rang tinny in his ears, and white spots danced across his vision. He put his head between his knees, and gripped the phone with both hands, willing Angel's daddy to hurry.

"This is Hank."

"Mr. Mur—" He tried to clear his throat, but couldn't get enough air.

"Aiden? Is that you?"

Lifting his shoulders, Aiden begged his lungs to fill.

"What's happened?" Mr. Murphy's voice rose in concern.

He hated to drag him into the mess, but he had no choice. "Yeah. I'm … hurt."

"Are you at home?"

"Ye—"

"I'll be there in five. Stay put."

Relief flooded his system, giving his brain the okay to check out. He briefly registered the words before he dropped the phone, tumbling sideways to the carpet.

———

Aiden's hearing was the first thing to reawaken. An air compressor, the phone ringing, metallic tapping, a few thick Irish accents battling for who was the loudest. All muffled like they were coming from a distance. Cracking open an eyelid, he recognized Hank's desk, and realized he was lying on the sofa in Angel's dad's office.

"You're back."

Mr. Murphy.

Aiden tried to lift his head, but apparently, it had morphed into a boulder during his blackout. Something cold was removed from his back, as Hank's tree-trunk legs moved into view.

"Now, don't you be trying to move. I've put salve on your back and a bandage or two, but you need to go careful. I'll help you sit up so you can swallow something for your pain."

He gasped as Hank maneuvered his body upright. It hurt like a bitch. His brain hovered about a foot above his head, and his stomach had collapsed in on itself. But other than that, he was ready for boot scootin'.

Curling his hands over the edge of the sofa cushion, he held himself upright while Hank popped the tablets in his mouth, and tipped some cool water down his throat. It soothed his thirst, but awakened his empty stomach. A loud gurgle escaped into the room.

"Ye hungry? I'll get Harvey to get you something."

"No, don't tell anyone. Please."

"Who do you think helped me carry you in here, lad? I didn't want to put pressure on your back, so he grabbed one end and I grabbed the other."

Aiden's face twisted, turning pink as he studied the carpet.

"Hey. You can always count on a Murphy to take care of you. We're not going to spread the word that your pa is a beast. Besides, he's doing a good enough job of starting gossip on his own."

"What do you mean?"

"Never mind, lad. I shouldn't have spoken ill of your kin." He patted the cushion, repositioning it for Aiden. "Lie back down on your side and let the medicine kick in. I've got a bucket here for you if you're likely to lose your lunch, but the food will be on its way shortly."

Aiden reached for the arm of the sofa, and eased his body down to the cushion. He didn't look at Mr.

Murphy. The look of pity on Hank's face was too much to bear. But what was worse, was knowing that his own father would never care for him like Hank did. And Hank would never be his father. If he could change one thing in his life, that would be it.

The pain slowly receded to a dull throb, and Aiden let go of the tension in his muscles. He listened to Hank shuffle some papers and tap on his keyboard, until the door swung open and Harvey, Hank's younger brother, barged in.

"Aiden. Good to see you're back in the room. Did you have a nice kip, ye lazy sod?" He dumped a paper bag in front of Aiden's face. "Got my lunch for you. Some quiche and salad from the missus. She tries to get me to eat the healthy stuff." He scoffed. "A man needs more sustenance than rabbit food and a bit of egg. She doesn't need to know I'll be swapping it for a burger. If you're still hungry after that, I'll get one for you, too." Harvey smoothed a hand over his red beard, looking pleased with himself.

"Thanks, Mr. Murphy. That's very generous of you."

"I keep telling you to call me Harvey. Mr. Murphy is this one here." He poked a large finger in Hank's direction. "He's the boss. I'm the talent."

Angel's daddy rolled his eyes. "Okay, Harvey. Thanks. Get out of here before you make the boy pass out again from all the hot air you're blowin'."

Harvey grinned and left, bumping shoulders with his older brother, Harry, as the man stood at the door.

"Are you okay there, son?" Harry's brow bunched in concern, smudged by grease and sweat. His large fist had a strangle hold on the door knob. Aiden worried he might snap it off.

Harry was the middle child of the three Irish brothers, and probably the most practical and level headed of the bunch. He ran the day-to-day operations in the workshop, and kept Hank's grand ideas in check.

"I'm feeling a bit better, thank you."

"Good to see you haven't lost your manners. I'll be back to check on you. Call me if you need me. Anytime." Harry eyeballed Aiden. "I mean it." The door knob rattled as he released it and shut the door behind him.

He was so damn lucky to have the Murphys in his life. What would he do without them? A shiver passed over Aiden's body and he swallowed against a tight throat.

Hank helped him up and he got to work on the food. Quiche had never tasted so good. He probably resembled a stray dog the way he was scoffing down the sustenance, but he didn't care.

Hank's discerning eye followed his every move. Worry flowed across the room in waves, wrapping him in an embrace he wouldn't be able to tolerate. He could feel the unvoiced questions prodding at him, and knew the man wouldn't hold them in forever. Hank wasn't stupid. He'd been suspicious of Aiden's home situation for a while. Sir was careful to put his marks where people wouldn't be able to see them. He'd ended up with a black eye once, but he blamed that on a stray baseball. The flat set of Mr.

Murphy's eyes and mouth told him the man wasn't buying his bullshit.

He sat staring at the empty container, his fork still gripped in one hand.

"Are you gonna talk to me, lad?"

"What is there to say?"

"Did he beat you because you were late for dinner, or was it because you were with us?"

"Both."

He heard a hiss of air escape Hank's nose. "There is no excuse for that behavior. Do you hear me?"

Aiden hung his head. Logically, he knew he didn't deserve the harsh treatment, but the little boy inside that wanted to please his father believed it was his fault. That he wasn't a good enough son.

"I don't care if you've gone and stolen a car. You'd be in the lockup, but you wouldn't be lying half dead, bleeding. I nearly took you to the medical center, but I knew that would do a number on your family life. I was a hair's breath away, lad. And one day, I'm afraid I'm not going to have a choice. I love you like my own. It kills me to have to leave you in harm's way. Give me the word and I'll report him."

Aiden rubbed his chin, his eyes shooting up to Hank's. He knew the man cared for him, but it was always a shock to hear the words out of his mouth. Out of anyone's mouth. Despite the rush of euphoria, he let the fear of his father override it. "I can't do that. He'll kill me."

"That's what I'm worried about."

"Please … don't." The words wheezed out as panic gripped his chest.

His father was a prominent member of the community. He owned a law firm in town and represented all the big names in the county, his sights firmly set on politics and Washington DC. Aiden didn't want to cause any dramas. He'd never live it down. Literally.

Mr. Murphy's lips set in a grim line, and the wrinkles on his brow cut deeper as he sat watching Aiden in silence.

Aiden put the container back in the bag to resist squirming. Hank was a formidable man. Aiden had never seen him get angry, but he had a way about him that stopped anyone from wanting to argue. Except Angel.

Aiden figured he wouldn't be seeing her for a few days. Fatigue settled on him like a lead apron. He let his eyes fall shut and felt the bag being tugged from his hands. A gentle push on his shoulder urged him to lie down. He was on board with that plan. There was no fight left. For now, he was safe and in Hank's care. That was all he could wish for. It would've been better if Angel could be by his side, but he didn't want her to know about his father. Didn't want to appear weak in her eyes.

He knew that if he looked in the mirror … that's what he'd see. Weakness.

Chapter Three

Angel held her glasses in her hand, squinting at the blurry figure in the mirror. She put the frames back on, blinking at her reflection, before lifting the glasses above her brow. Her eyelids narrowed again. No amount of squinting was going to make her eyesight improve, darn it. She dropped the glasses back on her nose and pushed her hair off her pale face.

Plain Jane.

Not that she could dress up her school uniform, but come on. She was sixteen, weren't things supposed to be changing? She religiously dyed her boring black hair to a more vivacious red, with the help of her cousins, who were all redheads blessed by nature and not the bottle. Her father had the same problem, being the only raven among his flame-haired brothers. But in his case, he preferred it that way.

She huffed and shifted her attention to her lack of chest, cupping each modest swell with a palm. She didn't look any older than thirteen. When would she start looking like a woman?

Angel's face twisted in a grimace. She wished she had her mother to talk to. Reaching out, she took a black and white photo from where it was wedged into the mirror frame. The image of her mother, beaming with a newborn Angel in her arms. She'd been a beautiful woman before her life was cut short by a drunk driver. The loss of her mother had unpacked its bags and settled in the core of her heart, a companion for life. It was times like this that it would twinge and throb, reminding her of what she'd never have again. Angel knew her aunts would help her out with anything she needed, but it wasn't the same.

She put the photo back in its spot next to the one of her and Aiden, taken when they were two years younger, while horsing around in her yard. Her body had awakened to him around that time. She'd always seen him as more than a friend, but right then, she was sure he wanted him. Angel wondered when his feelings had started to change, and what he really thought of her lack of assets.

She hadn't seen him at school the last two days, and her paranoid mind thought that maybe she had something to do with his absence. Her fingers twisted together. Maybe she'd scared him off by being too forward. Or maybe he didn't like her as much as she imagined. Untangling her fingers, she rubbed her bottom lip where her teeth had sunk in a little too hard, and reassured herself that he'd been just as into it as she had been. She'd felt his excitement in her hand. Well, more like squashed it under her hand. *Ugh.*

A loud tapping on the window made her jump with an embarrassing scream. She turned to find Aiden grinning at her through the glass. Forcing her shoulders to relax, Angel dashed over to push open the barrier.

"How long have you been there, spying like a psycho?"

He rested his elbows on the window ledge while the rest of him balanced on a sturdy elm branch, moving as it swayed in the breeze. He'd never climbed to her window before. Not that she knew of, anyways. She'd better be more careful about shutting the curtain.

"Only long enough to watch you … uh … look at the photo."

His eyes averted and her gut dropped, heat rushing up her neck. Oh, good Lord. He'd seen her feeling her boobs. She sucked in a breath, almost choking on her own spit.

Sh—ugar.

Lurching forward, she grabbed the window and yanked it closed, narrowly missing his elbow.

"Hey! What was that for?" Aiden's head bounced in and out of view, while his fingers struggled for purchase on the ledge.

"You saw!"

"Yeah, I saw. How was I supposed to know you'd be feeling yourself up? Are you coming down or do you need to assess yourself some more? We're gonna be late for school."

She growled, baring her teeth, but he just grinned back and started to climb down.

Pausing, he looked back up. "For the record, if you need a second opinion, I'd be happy to give one."

"Ooh, you cheeky—" She slammed her mouth shut before the curse escaped. "You won't be getting anywhere near them," she yelled through the glass. He'd descended out of sight, but his laugh reached her ears and tugged the corners of her mouth in a smile.

Picking up her bag, she bolted down the staircase to find Aiden and her daddy seated at the kitchen table, talking about baseball.

"Come on. We're going to miss the bus." She looked away from Aiden who was fighting a grin, and gave her father a tight hug. "Bye, Daddy. Love you big."

"Love you bigger. Enjoy your day, kids." He waved them off, cutting another slice of fried egg.

Sweat sprang from her pores as the sun bit down on her skin. Angel ducked under the cover of the trees lining the street, folding her hand into Aiden's when he offered it. She hummed and jiggled her hand in his. This was one of her favorite parts of the day. Sharing the trip to school with him. The day ahead held more promise when she got to start it by spending time with him. That's what love does.

Turning her attention to Aiden, she found him staring ahead, troubled thoughts creasing his brow.

"Isn't your dad working today?" Aiden's voice had an edge, making it squeakier than usual.

"No, he said he had some stuff to take care of."

"Oh." Aiden let his head fall forward and grabbed the strap of his bag, watching the ground as they walked to the stop.

He did that often. Retreated into his own head. She usually just waited patiently for him to work through whatever had him distracted and to come back to her. But there was something about the tight set of his jaw, and the grip he had on his bag, that had her concerned about where he'd retreated to today.

"So, where have you been the last few days?"

"Hm? Oh, I had to do some stuff for my father."

"Like what?" She used a playful tone to lighten the heaviness following him, but any mention of his father was a bad omen.

"Legal stuff that I can't tell you about, or you'd have to sign a gag order." His words were joking, but his face was grim.

"Ha. You wouldn't hurt me. You wouldn't hurt anyone." She tried for playful again, although she meant what she said.

"Not if I can help it."

The bus pulled up, letting out a loud hiss and screech as it stopped and let them on. They lived way out on the edge of town, so they had their pick of the seats with only a couple of other students already seated. Angel waved hello and Aiden gave a quiet nod as they made their way to the back. She plopped down in her usual spot by the window, and Aiden folded himself stiffly beside her. He normally dumped his bag under his feet, but today, he hugged it to him, hunching over it like he was protecting a wad of cash inside. He wasn't looking at her, either. He just fixed his eyes on the seat in front, and bounced his knee like a jack rabbit. She twisted her hands in her lap, wanting the sick feeling that was invading her stomach to go away.

His tawny gaze darted over her shoulder to watch the passing fields. "Are you comin' to watch ball practice after school?"

"Yeah. I'll be there, like I always am."

"Cool. Big game this weekend." He turned back to the front, stretching his neck to watch the road, she guessed.

What is going on?

Angel placed a hand on his shoulder, meaning to get him to relax, but he jerked away from her touch, hissing in a breath.

She snatched her hand away, her eyes levering wide. "You're hurt?"

"I hurt myself climbing your tree this mornin'. I shouldn't have done it. Sorry about that, by the way."

The bus pulled over, letting a few more students on, before pitching forward as it took off again.

"Let me see." She lifted the bottom of his shirt several inches before he tugged it out of her grip, snapping at her that he was fine.

She bit down on her lip, covering her mouth with a hand. She'd seen enough to know he wasn't fine at all. Angry red lashes that had turned into purple bruises, some of them deep enough to have scabbed over.

Legal stuff, huh? More like illegal.

"What really happened?" Her voice quivered, moisture gathering in her eyes because she'd already guessed the truth.

"Just leave it, Angel," he spat out the words, cutting her as deeply as he had been.

She loved this boy with all her heart. She wanted to help him and he wasn't having any of it.

"No. I can't."

"Yes. You can." His jaw clenched around the words.

"Don't push me away. There's no way I can stand by, knowing you're hurting like this."

"You can't help me. There's nothing anyone can do."

"Bullshit!" She twisted in the seat, leaning close so she could whisper-yell. "I can tell daddy and he can call the sheriff. You could come and live with us, we have plenty of spare rooms in that big old house. I can take care of you, and your daddy will be arrested. Probably your mama, too. Don't try and tell me she doesn't know what's going on. What kind of mama allows someone to hurt her baby? I don't care if it is your pa."

"My father is a lawyer. Don't you think he'd be able to find a way out of trouble? Who's gonna believe my word over his? He's friends with the sheriff. If I say anything, my life will get worse, not better." His eyes held a desperation that tore through her heart. "I'll become the sob story that no one can look in the eye, but everyone is happy to gossip about. The kids at school will make fun, or worse, not talk to me at all." He rested his palm over her clenched fist. "Come on, Angel, you can't fix this. Okay?"

She pushed up her glasses. "No. Not even close."

Angel spun away from him and focused on her hands fisted in her lap. She swiped angry tears away with her fingers, knowing some of his points were valid. If she could get proof that it was his father who'd done this, then the sheriff would have to take notice, and Aiden had a chance to get away.

"Your pa knows."

Her eyes jerked back to his and her lips parted to speak, but she couldn't sort through the mix of hope, betrayal, and defeat she was feeling, to form any words. If her daddy knew, why hadn't he done anything about it?

"He came to get me. Fixed me up. I've been recovering in his office and going home at night pretending I was fine, until I could go to bed. He phoned the school for me, too. Got that all squared away, somehow. If my father knew, he'd be causing all sorts of dramas for your pa. He'd try to, anyways. Your daddy has more power in this town than my father, and that drives him crazy. But it's not enough for people to believe such a serious accusation."

She turned away, wanting to cover her ears. Fields gave way to suburbia as the bus trudged on to school, stopping more frequently now. Angel stared at the houses thinking everything looked the same, but her stomach sank down to her knees with a feeling that nothing would be the same ever again. She could taste it on her tongue, like sour milk. She wanted to spit it out. She wanted to march right up to Mr. Thomas and spit and hiss, and kick his shins for what he'd done. What a brute of a man.

For the first time in her life, she thought she might be capable of hatred.

Chapter Four

Aiden flicked a loose piece of grass off his baseball shirt, and cautiously rolled his shoulders. His back throbbed like a thumb after a hammering, but he was happy. Ball practice was awesome. The guys were more than ready to face off against their rival team that weekend. His teammate's mama had dropped him and Angel a few blocks away, and now they strolled home, hands clasped.

"Did you see that catch?"

"Yeah. I also saw how you couldn't get up for two minutes after you landed. Why didn't you sit this one out?"

"Because I don't wanna make anyone suspicious, and I don't want to give my father the satisfaction of making me miss out on the good stuff."

She nodded. "Yeah, I appreciate that. But shouldn't you rest up before Saturday? How're you going to slide into home base if you've opened up all your cuts again?"

"I'll take an ice bath."

Angel pouted her cute mouth and looked up at him with those emerald eyes darkened by concern. He wrapped an arm around her shoulders and laid a firm kiss on her lips.

"I'll be fine."

"I wish I could believe you."

Dropping his bag, he moved in front of her, blocking her way. He took her face into his hands. "I'll be fine."

Again, his lips captured hers, lingering for a good long taste this time. Angel's hand landed on his chest and smoothed their way to his neck, leaving a path of heat in their wake. Damn, this girl was his drug. He'd endure anything as long as he didn't have to be apart from her. He shifted his grip to her waist and angled his head for a deeper kiss. He had to taste her fully, licking into her mouth. Aiden was careful not to push her. He wanted to pull her body into his and obliterate the space between them. But they were on the street, and if either of their father's saw, there'd be hell to pay. He pulled back, gently setting her away, and smirking at the way she swayed on her feet when he let her go to pick up his bag.

Grabbing her hand, he continued walking, rounding the corner of their street. As always, his eyes found the big, beautiful, antebellum masterpiece that had been in Angel's family for generations. Its blue shutters stood out against the white walls, proud columns marking its entrance. Grand oak trees protected the street in a canopy of green, as they walked closer to the bend that would reveal his modest, plantation-plain style home.

Angel's feet slowed to a stop, her arm tugging his behind him. He looked back in question. He didn't think her ivory skin could get any paler, but she was whiter than his uniform. Her eyes held a disbelief and panic that had his head whipping around to see what was going on.

"No. Mother fucker. No." He dropped Angel's hand and sprinted towards his house.

Two bulky removal guys carried his desk into the back of their truck. Another two followed with his bed. Aiden forgot about the pain in his back as a surge of rage-fueled adrenaline took over. He stopped across the street, raking his fingers through his hair and pulling hard at the roots. They'd cleaned out most of the furniture already.

"Fuck!" He squatted down, gripping his head, eyes fixed on his uncertain future, and the worst hell on Earth packed into the back of that truck.

He searched for his father's car, not finding any sign of it. The asshole was probably screwing over his employees' 401K retirement plans.

Angel stepped into his view, clutching at his shirt. "We can run away. Daddy will understand." She yanked on the material, sobbing. "You can borrow Daddy's bike. Let's go."

They ran back to Angel's place. She darted up the stairs to grab a backpack and some clothes, while he raided the cupboards for food. His hands shook so badly that he smashed a jar of jelly, the red mush on the floor demonstrating the state of his heart.

"Fuck!"

He zipped his bag and rubbed a hand over his face as Angel came back down. "Where are we going to go? Have you got enough money for a bus fare? Is there even a bus out of town at this time of day?"

"I've got it all planned. We can hide out at Saunders' Hardware. You know he has an apartment above the store. I know where he keeps the key. We can't use the bus, that'll be the first place they'll look. It's too late to ride anywhere, but we'll have to leave early in the morning and take the back roads to the next county. We'll hitch a ride as soon as we can. I found Daddy's emergency stash. That should get us food for a while until we can get work. I have some savings, too."

"Are you sure about this, Angel? You don't have to leave everything for me."

"You stupid boy. You are everything. Don't you know that by now?"

Adrenaline punched into his system at hearing her words, and he shuffled his weight, not knowing how to let it seep in deep where he needed it. Love wasn't a familiar term. He knew he loved her. He'd hoped she felt the same. But, belief and acceptance didn't come easily for his battered heart.

Her eyes moved around the room, taking it all in through a sheen of tears. "Let's go before someone finds us."

Aiden swallowed past the guilt lodged in his throat, feeling like a selfish asshole for letting her do this, but unable to contemplate a life without her. He gathered her in his arms, absorbing her strength, knowing he'd never be man enough to deserve the sacrifice she was making for him.

As her body dissolved into grief in his embrace, he let himself go there with her, sliding his back down the kitchen cupboard until they joined the jelly puddle on the floor.

Of all the pain his father had inflicted over the years ... this was the worst. He'd outdone himself. What kind of assholes were his grandparents to have raised such a heartless bastard? Old money from New Hampshire, that much he knew. They had a lot to answer for.

He pulled Angel against him, breathing her in and shutting his eyes. The asshole gene had to stop with his father. Aiden was going to do everything to become man enough to repay her loyalty and love. He'd get them safely away. Somehow.

———

Gravel sprayed behind their tires as they rode into the alleyway the next block over from the hardware store. Out of breath, Angel hopped off the bike, her thighs burning from the long ride. Her eyes darted everywhere, hoping not to see any familiar faces. They'd taken the most convoluted path they could, making it to the center of town by late afternoon. Most people had gone home for the day, with only a few stragglers moving about.

"Here, behind the dumpster. This is a good place to hide the bikes."

Aiden waved Angel over into the god-awful cloud of stench wafting from the giant metal trash can. She held her breath, shoving her bike behind his, before she jogged to the end of the alleyway and back to clean air.

She sucked in a cleansing breath. "Well, that was foul. There's something brewing in there and it ain't sweet tea."

"I think there's a family of feral cats using it as a latrine." Aiden pinched his nose. Not that it would help. "Okay, what's the plan?"

"I'll distract him while you ..." Angel's finger landed on his chest. "... get the key. It hangs on a nail underneath the counter next to the register. Look for a red keyring in the shape of an apple. You can't miss it."

She spun around and poked her head into the street. They had to move fast to catch Mr. Saunders before he locked up for the night. "Okay, the coast is clear." She casually walked up the street and into the store, spotting Mr. Saunders' head behind the counter. Aiden ducked into the shelves, silently moving his way to the back of the store, while she headed up the middle aisle.

"Hi, Mr. Saunders. How're ya doin'?" Pasting on a smile, she rested her hands on the countertop to stop them from trembling.

"Well, if it isn't Angel Murphy. you're lookin' more like your mama every time I see ya. I'm doin' fine. How can I help you?"

She always expected him to talk with an Irish accent, he looked so much like a leprechaun. Especially now that his hair was turning white at the front, and he was so short that she had no trouble looking him in the eye.

Pursing her lips half in thought and half to stop the giggle, she tapped a finger on her bottom lip. "I need a new adjustable wrench for my daddy. He broke his favorite one and he's been a bear with a sore head ever since. Do you know what brand he uses?"

"Oh, yeah. I make sure to keep his preferred tools in stock. They make 'em tough, but your daddy puts his tools through their paces with those vehicles he builds. I got 'em right over here."

He tottered off, explaining the difference between a few brands to no one in particular. Angel waited until she saw Aiden duck behind the register, before she followed Mr. Saunders.

"This here is the one your daddy likes to use." He held the shiny tool, wearing a triumphant smile.

"Yeah, that looks familiar. Could you keep it aside for me? I'd like to give it to him as an early Father's Day present."

"Absolutely. No problem. Do you want me to organize gift wrapping for you? I don't normally do that sort of thing, but I can make an exception for you and your daddy."

"That's mighty generous of you, Mr. Saunders, but I can do that myself. Thank you so much for your help, I appreciate it." *More than you know.*

"All right, young lady. Pleasure doin' business with ya. I'll see you soon."

No, you won't. Her throat burned with the need to cry. She nodded and walked out, ordering her legs not to run and her tears to back down. God, she'd just lied to one of the sweetest, most honorable men she knew. Her eyes checked the sky for storm clouds as she stepped onto the street, expecting a bolt of lightning to strike her down. She saw nothing but the oncoming dusk, and Aiden holding the side door to the apartment open in the alleyway.

Ducking in after him, she locked the door behind her and tiptoed up the dark staircase to their hideaway.

One big room was broken into four parts. The kitchen and bathroom occupied the two back corners, and the dining and living area sat across the front, looking out at the street. The apartment was only half as deep as the store below. She guessed there must be a storeroom behind the back wall, built over the back half of the store.

"Hello, 1970's. The Brady Bunch called, they want their set back." Aiden shielded his face with his hands.

She couldn't stop the giggle. The orange and brown color scheme was kind of offensive. *And ... shag pile. Really?*

"Decorating is not his strong suit, that's for sure. I don't see a bed. That must be a foldout sofa. We have to be thankful we have a place to bunk down until we can figure out how to get away."

"I know, and I am, so thankful. I was just trying to lighten the mood." He came over to her, encircling her in his arms. "You're so amazing. I can't believe that you would drop everything to be with me. I'm still in shock that this is happening."

"Me, too."

His intense gaze roved across her face. She was covered in a sheen of sweat and dried tears, and was probably the color of a beetroot. She got the impression that she could be covered in grease, and he'd still find her beautiful. He locked her in his arms like he wanted to hold her forever. They'd been forced into this situation, but the thought of them running away together was becoming more and more appealing. Sharing meals, sharing a home, sharing a bed ... She guessed Aiden's mind had gone there, too, because he tilted his hips back, discretely adjusting his stance to hide his body's response to the possibilities.

He cleared his throat. "We need to get cleaned up."

She almost pulled him closer, but through the dividing wall came a banging and scraping, like Mr. Saunders was moving stuff around.

"Sh. Did you hear that?"

Aiden's arms went stiff around her. She felt his heartbeat thundering through his chest and into hers.

"We can't run the water until we know he's gone home." Aiden's breath puffed over her ear as he whispered the words, and she nodded in assent.

It had been a risk, to involve Mr. Saunders. As soon as the call to search went out, he'd be able to tell people that he'd seen them. They would have to search the apartment. Angel just hoped they could get away before that happened. The prickling along her skin told her they didn't have a chance. She burrowed into Aiden's chest willing her fears away, and taking as much time in his arms as she could.

———

They waited an hour for Mr. Saunders to pack up and leave, watching through the curtains as his car disappeared down the street, before they took turns in the shower. They figured if they used the light from the open bathroom, they could see enough without alerting anyone on the street of their presence. From her seat at the table, Angel eyed Aiden in the kitchen, gathering ingredients for their dinner. His body was almost completely engulfed by one of her father's T-shirts, his school shorts hidden under its length, making it look more like a dress. Aiden was tall, much taller than her, but her father was a giant. He could always tuck it in, she figured. It was better than wearing his uniform. People would be looking for that.

"I got the peanut butter, but I smashed the jelly jar. Sorry." He sent her a sheepish smile.

"That's okay. Peanut butter is delicious on its own."

The truth was, she wasn't all that hungry. Her attention was half on the door, waiting for Mr. Thomas to barge in. Deep in the pit of her gut, she knew it was going to happen. If not here, then somewhere down the road. He would find them. The man would track his son to the end of the Earth.

"Here ya go." The plate clattered on the wooden table and Aiden took a seat beside her. "How mad do you think your daddy will be when he figures out we've disappeared together?"

Picking bits off the crust, she rubbed them between her fingers, making a pile of crumbs. "Spitting mad, but not at us. He'll see the removal truck and figure out that we had no choice." She brushed the crumbs off her fingers and leaned back in the chair. "I don't get it. Why didn't they tell you about the move? It's like they're runnin' from something."

"That's what I don't understand. Unless he's been planning this for a while, and kept me in the dark on purpose just to be an asshole." Aiden dropped his uneaten sandwich and pushed his plate away. "Do you have any idea how we're gonna get out of here?"

Angel pushed the hair off her face with a sharp exhale. "Well, I know one thing. We're going to have to sneak out of here under the cover of darkness. Every person with eyes will be looking for us."

"Shit. Angel, I'm so sorry to put you through this."

"Hush. It's not your fault at all. I'm truly sorry that your father is such an ass."

Aiden's eyebrows shot up. "Did you just cuss?"

"Sure did. I think the situation warrants it."

"That means you owe me a kiss." His hand made a come-hither gesture. "Pay up."

Shoving her chair back, Angel stood in front of his chair, and placed her hands on his shoulders, leaning down for a quick peck on the lips. As she straightened, Aiden took her hand in his, entwining their fingers. The humor leeched out of his light brown eyes, replaced by despair.

Angel's legs suddenly felt boneless and she twisted sideways to sit on his lap, wrapping her arms around his shoulders, and burying her face in his chest as tears flooded her eyes.

"Hey." He smoothed a hand down her spine. "Hey, hey. We're going to get through this."

"This is our goodbye … You know it." She swiped at her cheeks a little too forcefully.

"No, don't say that. There's hope. Isn't there? There's got to be hope for us."

"Aiden—"

"No. Don't. I can't—" Intense pain shaded his eyes before his mouth dropped to cover hers in a desperate kiss. "Don't."

He framed her face with his hands, eyes darting over all her features. She must look a fright, but he watched her with a reverence … like she really had descended from heaven. Like he wanted to drink in this moment before it drained away.

She did the same, taking in every inch of his skin. The soft stubble he'd only started shaving a year and a half ago. His strong, honey-blonde brows drawn low over tawny eyes. The tension in his shoulders, layered with more muscle now that he was nearly a man. She'd never get to see him fully grown, but she knew he'd be so gorgeous. On top of his beautiful soul, the combination would be addictive to females. Another woman would undoubtedly snap him up.

She tried to swallow against the panic gripping her throat. Blinking up at him through wet lashes, she bit her lips. There was one thing she could give him. It was always meant to be his, and he could give her the same in return. She licked her lips, mouth suddenly dry with nerves.

They could be each other's first.

"Aiden. Make love to me."

His eyes popped wide, his hands twitching on her face. "What?"

"You heard me. I need you."

"Angel, you're … It's only because of the situation, you wouldn't be ready otherwise. I don't want to rush things because we're scared or desperate, or whatever."

"God, Aiden! If they find us and I never get to show you what you mean to me, I swear I'll never forgive you."

"But."

"Nope." She leaned back and ripped off her T-shirt.

His sharp exhale washed across her chest. "Oh, my God." Aiden's hands gripped her thighs, and the wooden chair creaked as he pushed back to get a better view.

Angel should have been self-conscious. She wasn't. She was triumphant at the heavy-lidded look he was giving her, and the hardness growing under her thigh. Reaching down, she took hold of the hem of his shirt and tugged up. He shook his head, snapping himself out of his daze, before his arms jerked it off and a smile broke out on his face.

"God, you're so beautiful." Aiden raised a hand, hovering over her skin as his eyes shot back to hers. "Can I … can I touch you?"

"Please," she breathed.

Smoothing his palm over her collar bone, he ran it softly over her cotton covered breast. Her nipples peaked in welcome at the tingly sensation, as his other palm gave equal attention to the other side. Encasing her ribcage in his grip, he tugged her forward so he could take her lips again. Each stroke drew them closer, merging their hearts as one even as the clock ticked in the background, signaling the countdown to the end. She wanted to scream at the injustice of it all, and melt at the sensations he was inducing at the same time. The emotional clash had her trembling, and hauling in the heady air between them. One thing was for sure … this felt right. She was ready for this. They'd known each other for most of their lives. Were entrenched in each other's heart and soul. This *was* right.

Aiden stood, maneuvering her legs so they circled his waist, and carried her to the sofa. Leaning down, he laid her on the soft cushion, before the weight of him nestled in the cradle of her legs. Wrapping his arms under her back, he continued to drug her with his kiss, his tongue venturing out to taste and take more with each thrust. Angel squirmed under him, trying to get closer and ease the ache growing in her center.

His head jerked up and she took a moment to focus on the fierce look on his face.

Pulling his arms out from under her, he sat back. "I want to see you." He fiddled with the frayed edge of her shorts. "All of you."

She looked down her body, watching her fingers fumble with the button and zipper as her chest heaved for breath. Aiden helped her out by smoothing his hands down her torso and legs, taking the shorts with him. She heard the heavy fabric hit the shag pile, before his hands returned, caressing their way back up to her hips. She lifted her hips, giving him the okay to take off her panties. His groan vibrated through her belly where he dropped a kiss, spurring her blood to race impossibly faster.

"Now you," she panted as she ditched her bra.

He nearly lost balance as he pushed himself to stand, eager to shuck the nuisance fabric.

The shorts dropped, leaving him in his boxers, his erection straining behind the fabric and peeking out the top. A mix of thrill and fear buzzed under her skin and in her stomach. That thing was bigger than she expected. How the heck was this going to work?

"You look a little scared." His face was pained and unsure. "I don't want to scare you. I'll leave my shorts on." He bent down to pick them up.

"No. I want to see you, too."

"Are you sure? I won't do anything you don't want me to. We don't have to do this at all."

He was killing her with his determination to be sweet and considerate. She looked away to gather some patience, spotting the shiny red apple keyring on the kitchen counter. She was going to have to channel her inner Eve if she was going to tempt him with her fruit.

"Sweet Jesus, Aiden, ditch the underwear."

He snorted and ripped them down like his life depended on it. She watched his shaft bounce free, certain that thing wouldn't fit in her. Her fingers itched to touch. Sitting up, she watched his mouth drop open as she reached out a hand. His stomach muscles jerked when she made contact with soft skin over hard flesh. With her fingers wrapped around his girth, she enjoyed the feel of him and the way he panted in excitement. Her core tightened in response.

Aiden dropped to his knees on the carpet, placing his palm on her belly and his lips on her hip. She leaned back on her hands, unsure of what he was up to, but willing to wait and see. Her thighs slid together, moistened by her arousal. Heat rose from her chest to her cheeks at her predicament, and she prayed that she wasn't ruining the sofa cushion. Aiden's fingers started to move south, through trimmed dark curls to where she needed him.

"Holy shit …" His gaze shot to hers, sending her a rueful smile. "Sorry. It's just, you're—"

His thumb slicked down through her wetness, and his voice broke on a strangled groan. His other hand urged her to part her legs, to give him more room. To trust him with the most private part of her. She obliged, relaxing her muscles and letting her knees fall apart. There was no room for shame under the protection of his love. His touch sent shivers of heat over her skin and sent her blood pulsing. Her center grew greedy for the feel of him. She started to rock her hips to his rhythm. When he leaned down to suck a nipple into his mouth, she fell back on her elbows, pushing her chest out to give herself to him.

Aiden's hand encircled her breast, pushing it up into his mouth so he could take more.

"Ow, not so hard."

"Shit. Sorry." He pulled his arm back. "I'm new at this."

"Yeah. I know. Just go gentle to start with, okay?"

"Okay."

He leaned down again and kissed her breast, before burying his face in her stomach and inhaling.

"Can I hold you?" The words rasped out of his throat.

Angel scooted against the backrest to make room. "That would be nice."

Aiden stretched out beside her, tucking her into his chest. His fingers danced along her spine, her hip, and back up her stomach. Sparks shot along in their wake, as his tongue tangled with hers. She let her hands roam, too. Memorizing the planes and dips of smooth skin and taut muscle. Angel's breath hitched when his fingers found her center again. She hooked a leg over his hip and anchored her hands flat on his chest, as he took her on a journey she'd never been on. Her brain switched off. She became a mass of sensations, and everything tightened and pulsed, building to something new and amazing. The mewling sounds escaping her throat surely couldn't have been her, but there was no way of stopping them. She needed more.

Looking him in the eye, she pleaded, "Aiden. I need ..."

His hand responded by pressing harder and picking up speed.

Eyelids dropping closed, she practically purred. "Mm."

"Ah, God, Angel."

Her butt cheek was caught in a deliciously rough grasp, as his mouth dipped to suck on her chest. His fingers didn't stop and the sparks of sensation built to a massive wave of pleasure, breaking out from her core. She bucked and shook, crying out in ecstasy. Angel had to grip his wrist to get him to stop. It was too much. she couldn't take anymore.

She tried to catch her breath, falling limp and unclenching her jaw. Her eyes opened to find Aiden's triumphant grin.

"Wow. I made you come."

"Come?"

"You know. Orgasm."

"Yeah. You did." She patted a hand over his heart, feeling cheated that she'd never get to experience that with him again.

"I want to do that again."

"I want to give you the same."

His hips bucked forward so his erection slid through her folds, drawing out a shudder from her still sensitive body. Her eyes rolled back before her lids sank down. She hooked her leg a bit higher and wrapped an arm around his back, reveling in the rasp of her nipples against his chest.

"I want to be inside you."

"Yes. Please."

"Yes?"

"Mm hm." She nodded, watching his expression flare with heat.

Her body roared to life with the thundering in her veins, anticipation tightening every muscle. He pushed up on one arm, and gave her hip a nudge to lie flat. She positioned herself, making room for him between her legs. Reaching for him, she dragged her hands down his back as he pressed his weight down, lining himself up with her entrance. He pushed down, fumbling to get the angle right as he figured out her body. She arched her back to help him out.

Angel willed herself to relax, and tried to even out her breathing. But, she remembered some overheard conversation in the girl's restroom, about how it would hurt the first time, and her lungs wouldn't obey. They pumped air like a bellows.

His hardness stretched her tender tissue and she tilted her chin up, fixing her eyes on the pleasure playing across Aiden's features to forget her discomfort. She wanted this with him. Wanted to be his, always.

Aiden's pupils threatened to engulf the whiskey color of his eyes, and his lips parted on a moan. She hooked her legs around his waist, and her belly turned liquid as he pushed further.

Feeling the pinch inside her, she dug her fingers into his back with a gasp, and pushed her face into his shoulder.

Aiden froze. "Are you okay?"

She bobbed her head, keeping her face firmly planted in his skin so she could take in his smell, and hide her reaction. "Mm. Just give me a second."

He started to pull back, but she locked her ankles, making him stay put.

"You're not okay."

"I will be. Please don't stop. I want to give you this."

"Okay." He didn't sound so sure.

His hand came up to stroke her hair and she felt the press of his lips on the crown of her head. On a long exhale, Angel rested back on the cushion and pulled back her nails, stroking his back to soothe both their pain. Leaning on an elbow, Aiden smiled down at her and feathered kisses over her face. His hand roamed up and down her body, lingering over her breasts and hips, stoking the flame of desire back to life.

She moaned and squeezed her legs, lifting her hips to get closer. The pain receded to a dull throb that whispered of pleasure. Aiden inched forward, obviously still unsure, but maybe needing to be closer, too.

The slide of his flesh against her inner walls was so new and overwhelming, and yet so addictive it had her panting for more. Their hips bucked and slapped together, gaining momentum quickly, as another wave of sensation slowly built.

She whimpered as the rhythm of Aiden's movements quickened, and his face twisted in exquisite agony. He jerked one last time, arching his back with one long, low groan, before he collapsed on top of her. His pulsing shaft tugged at her core, bringing her down before she fell off the ledge. She didn't care. Angel wrapped her limbs around him to enjoy their connection for as long as she could. Being able to bring him pleasure was the greatest high.

He lifted his head. "Sorry, I couldn't hold off any longer. You felt too good."

"So did you."

"Am I squashing you?"

She pulled him closer. "No. I like feeling your weight on me."

A dazzling smile cracked his face wide open, before he pressed his lips to hers, tasting the truth of her words.

"I love you. So much."

He didn't have to say it. She felt it deep in her soul, but it was nice to hear it anyways.

"I love you, too. Have since the beginning."

"Since the beginning." He nodded and sat up. "Let's get cleaned up and fold out the bed. We need to rest if we're gonna get up before the sun."

She didn't think they'd make it that far, but she wanted to enjoy sleeping, snuggled in his arms, just this once. If that was all she was going to get, she'd take it. She wasn't going to think about the future, because if she did, she'd crumble into a million pieces.

Now, she had some clue to the depths of pain her father had suffered when her mama passed away. She couldn't believe it was happening to her at the age of sixteen.

How would she live without him?

Chapter Five

Pounding. There was a pounding in her head.

Cool air rushed over her body as the warm blanket of Aiden's body left, as he bolted off the mattress. She shook her head and swung her legs to the side to sit up.

"Hold your dang horses, Thomas. Move outta the way so I can unlock the door before ya break it."

That's Mr. Saunders. Well, shit.

She aimed her fuzzy vision on the glowing hands of the clock above the table. 2:15 a.m., or close enough. Aiden faced the door, his body grim and stretched taut like the zombie apocalypse waited on the other side. In reality, what they were about to face was just as scary.

The door sprang open, dang near ripped off its hinges, as Aiden's father hurled himself into the room.

Raising an accusing finger, his fierce eyes shot daggers at Aiden. "Boy, you won't be able to breathe by the time I'm done with you. I hope you enjoyed your fun. Party's over, you're coming with me."

"No," Aiden gritted out.

Watching the face off through a deluge of tears, Angel sucked cool air between her teeth and gripped the edge of the bed to control her trembling. This was really happening. Now, she wanted to pinch herself awake. Her worst nightmare was happening before her eyes.

Mr. Thomas coughed out a humorless laugh. "I could have sworn you just disobeyed me, but my boy knows not to do that, or I'll beat the ever-loving shit out of him." He took a menacing step forward. "Why don't you try that again?"

"Brent. Back off. They're just kids."

Angel hugged herself at the sound of her daddy's voice. Leaning forward, she saw the glow of his blue eyes in the shadows of the stairwell. She knew he wasn't happy at finding them there, but concern seemed to outweigh the anger in his features.

"Stay out of this, Murphy. If it wasn't for your little whore, we wouldn't be in this situation."

"She's not a whore!" Aiden spat at his father.

Her daddy's heavy boot thumped on the shag pile as his rage spilled into the room. "How dare you. I understand you're mad, but watch your mouth, or I'll rearrange it for you."

"And I'll have you up on assault charges quicker than you can blink."

Two fists furled at her daddy's sides just waiting to hit their target. "You're a maggot. Praise the Lord that you're leaving town. You should leave Aiden here. This is where he belongs. He sure as hell doesn't belong with you."

"He's my son! Mine. He'll follow in my footsteps, not some grease monkey's. You're not taking him from me." Mr. Thomas rounded on Aiden, locking a hand around his bicep. "Come. Now."

"No. I'm not going."

She sat, a frozen block of ice, watching Aiden fight a tug of war between his heart and his duty. He seemed so much like the five-year-old boy she'd coaxed out of hiding on the day they met. Her heart wanted to break out of her chest and beat at his feet, so that he knew it would always be his.

"The hell you're not."

Mr. Thomas heaved his son's weight forward and Aiden fell to his knees. His head whirled around, his terrified gaze seeking hers.

"No!" She lunged forward, clinging on to him with all her strength. Her neck wrenched back as her hair was caught in the brute's grip.

The heavy smack of her daddy's fist hitting Mr. Thomas' jaw vibrated all the way down through her scalp before he let go of her.

"Angel." Aiden steadied her in his embrace while he watched his father hit the carpet.

"I'm okay." She gripped his shoulders, sobbing, knowing their efforts were futile. "I love you. Please never forget that."

His hair fell over his eyes, as he shook his head like he was trying to wake from a nightmare. "I won't. I love you more than life."

Mr. Thomas pushed to his feet, rubbing his jaw. He aimed a glare at her daddy, his face feral as he spat blood at his feet.

"Angel. Come on lass. Let him go now." Her daddy moved to shield her from further harm. "Lay a hand on my daughter again and I'll have you arrested."

"I've already called the sheriff." Mr. Saunders stood back in the kitchen watching her life fall to pieces.

She didn't know what to do. She didn't want to let go, but knew it was hopeless to hold on. She was only making things worse.

"Come on lass. I won't have you getting hurt."

"He's right, Angel." Aiden coaxed her back. "I'll be okay."

"I don't believe you." Bunching her T-shirt in her fists between her breasts, she prayed for the muscle beneath to hold together.

"Aargh, enough! We're done here."

Yanked to his feet, Aiden stumbled after his father, who stomped and cursed a path to the door. Aiden didn't take his eyes off her, locking a white-knuckled hand on the door frame to allow him one last silent goodbye, before his father pulled him out of sight. The last she heard was his hoarse cry and a thumping against the walls of the stairwell. That evil brute was hurting him.

She crushed the shirt beneath her hands, half expecting blood to start pouring between her fingers, from the gaping wound in her chest. Her shoulders heaved as she struggled for air, legs prickling with pins and needles where they lay folded under her weight.

Her daddy's strong arms wrapped her up in an embrace meant to be comforting, but not even he would be able to hold her together. He'd mended so many hurts with his hugs. They were magic. Even her mama's death had been made a tiny bit easier to endure within the envelope of her daddy's arms. She feared nothing would be able to put her back together after this. Nothing but Aiden walking back through that door. Or maybe waking up to find herself back on that hideous orange sofa bed, lying in Aiden's arms after they'd made love.

"Here are the keys. Take your time. I'll deal with the sheriff. Sorry, Angel." The door clicked shut as Mr. Saunders left.

"Angel. Sweetheart. Let's go home. We'll get him back. I promise. I'll do whatever it takes to get our boy back."

"How, Daddy?"

"Whatever it takes, lass."

She blinked at him, her vision blurring behind a cascade of tears and bursts of white. She thought his mouth moved, but the message was drowned out by the ringing in her ears.

This can't be real. This can't be real.

The room tilted as her daddy hefted her into his arms, her head lolling on her shoulders. A hint of red reminded her that the apple keyring still sat innocently in the kitchen, taunting her of dreams unfulfilled. The ruse of the promise of Eden ... before being cast out.

This morning she'd woken up a girl in love, and now she was a shattered woman.

Whatever it takes, lass.

She could only hope.

Titles by J. M. Adele

Coming Home Series

Shattered Home
Remembering Home
Finding Home
Leaving Home (Coming 2019)
Coming Home (TBA)

Sensing Series

Sensing You
Convincing You (Coming Soon)
Indulging You (TBA)

Bloodlust Series

Ashes and Dust
Ember and Flame

Excerpt from
Remembering Home

Chapter One

Self-hatred was the purest thing Aiden Thomas had felt in years. He stood in the bathroom of his hotel room, harsh, fluorescent light casting unforgiving shadows over the angles of his face. His shoulders wrenched up and down as each breath grew harder to drag in. The face reflected in the mirror twisted with shame and a fierce disgust. Black eyes bored into the mirror and back again in an infinite battle of wills and intimidation.

The news he'd discovered ten minutes ago was the baseball bat to the head he needed. A wakeup call after more than a decade of numb oblivion, isolation and ignorance. Aiden had let everyone down, including himself. He'd never see Hank Murphy again because he'd been behaving like a chicken shit, little boy. His teeth made a horrible grinding sound as he clenched his jaw.

The urge to destroy proved irresistible. He pounded his fist into the grim reflection, the shattering of the glass deafening in the small space. A satisfied smile crossed his face as he inspected his shredded knuckles. Aiden flexed his hand watching red spill down between his fingers, coloring the shards in the sink. It hurt like a bitch, and it felt fucking awesome.

The pussy in the mirror was gone. Aiden Thomas was awake and determined to make things right.

———

Almost a day later, he stood deliberately separate from a huddle of black sorrow, listening to the somber tones of a man of God eulogizing and offering prayer. A summary of the life of a man who meant so much to him, the one a young Aiden wished had been his real father.

The intermittent breeze carried away the murmurings of the minister, stirring the rich smell of freshly dug soil mixed with the more delicate scent of the floral adornment on the coffin. He sucked in the smells and the moisture in the southern air, grateful for some relief from the heaviness of his guilt. Beneath a makeshift bandage, his throbbing hand reminded him of the task ahead.

Aiden surveyed the crowd, recognizing most of his fellow mourners, although they were much older now. As a boy, he'd thought of them as his family until his father had disabused him of the notion, called him a foolish leech, and taught him that the only person he could truly rely on was himself.

He belonged to nobody.

All utter bullshit. He *had* belonged to Hank, his true father in every way that counted. He knew that now. Now that it was too late.

Jesus, Hank. I'm so sorry.

He set his jaw to prevent an agonized shout from escaping, as his eyes locked on the coffin. He forced them away, tilting his head side to side to loosen his neck. The pain from flexing his fingers allowed him to center his torment as far away from his heart as he could get it. It was welcome relief, however brief.

Aiden absorbed the poignant words, and looked around the gathering once again. A petite woman across from him drew his eyes. The only points of color were her red lips, and the green leaves and stem of a white rose visible through a curtain of raven hair. Each tear caught on the corner of her mouth before it trickled down her chin and fell to the earth. Her gloved hands clasped those of a fellow mourner's, obviously her close friend. They presented a striking contrast, a dark crown beside platinum blond. The women rocked slightly side-to-side, alternating between supporters and supported.

Something about the brunette pinched at his distant memories, imploring him to remember a familiarity long forgotten. Aiden's feet wanted to move of their own accord, to circle the huddle to get to her with some amount of stealth. He locked his knees refusing to bow to their demand, dropping his gaze to take in the grass beneath his feet. That'd be a good start. Embarrassing himself the first time he'd seen these people in fifteen years, and at the funeral of one of the town's most loved. His shoulders dropped as he pushed a long breath out, before raising his eyes once more.

The woman stood trembling, staring straight at him, barely holding it together. She was beyond beautiful, although agony etched her features. Her distressed state tugged at his protective side more than it should have, drawing the corners of his mouth down. Her big, doe-shaped eyes blinked through her tears, draining more rapidly now. Mouth quivering, her distress seemed to grow as she watched him. Jesus, she looked like she was going to collapse.

Aiden's right foot lifted and he stumbled forward slightly, catching himself before he could go any further. A prickle of awareness caused his stare to shift, taking in the narrowed gaze of her friend as she gripped onto her companion around the waist. He schooled his features, and quickly turned away. What the hell did he think he'd be able to do for her anyway?

Once again facing the Minister, he joined in the last prayers for his dear friend. "Rest in peace, old man," he said to himself, letting his grief wash over him once again. The minister finished the service and the coffin was lowered. A tepid breeze carried some dry leaves to join his friend in his final resting place in the ground.

Aiden watched as the woman broke away from her friend to throw a folded piece of paper and the rose onto the coffin. She made her way straight to him, stopping when the toes of their shoes tapped together, sending a jolt of adrenaline straight into his blood stream. He looked down at her leaning his shoulders away. *The fuck?* The closeness was jarring. Did she recognize him?

Her face tipped up, presenting him with her tear-stained beauty once more. Aiden pulled out a hanky from his jacket and offered it, needing to comfort her somehow.

"Thank y—" A sniffle and a gasp cut off her words. "... ou."

"Sorry for your loss." The rumble of his voice sounded deep as the inane words tumbled out of his mouth. He cringed inwardly. What could he say that didn't sound trite? *Hank would know what to say.*

Aiden's brown eyes drilled into her vivid green ones. She was an ethereal beauty. It was heartbreaking to witness the sadness pouring out of such perfection. Her head bobbed as she curled an unsteady hand around her throat, and burst into sobs.

"Oh sh—" He grimaced, raising a cautious hand to pat her on the shoulder. In response, she stepped into his side, grabbing onto the lapel of his jacket. Her jerky movements sent shock waves racing through his veins, the weight of her grip seeping into his bones. His mind blanked for a minute as his body took over. He shook his head to set his synapses scrambling, trying to make sense of this bizarre interaction.

When he arrived this morning, it sure didn't equate to a feeling of homecoming. He shouldn't have been surprised at the feeling of displacement and disconnection. That shit was pretty standard. But, this was Alabama.

Where he grew up. The only place that had ever felt like home. Now? Sweet home Alabama? Not so much. Standing with his arm around this stranger … this felt more like home. Aiden's eyes almost crossed from system overload. His body hadn't really *felt* anything in so long. He was used to living the life of an international nomad, roaming between photo shoots. His only interactions with others coming from behind a camera lens.

What the hell is happening?

The woman's shudders slowly lessened to the softer, rise and fall of her chest, as she breathed deeply in acceptance of his comfort. *Huh.* He had been able to offer something after all. It speared his soul, connecting him to another in a way he had forgotten existed. His breathing slowed in time with hers, every inhale drawing her delicate, jasmine perfume, and the scent of salty tears. Aiden was drawing as much comfort as he was giving, the exchange probably weighing more heavily in his favor. In a moment of tortured surrender, this petite woman had made him see how lonely he was.

Loneliness was his MO.

His life sucked.

Goddamn.

It made him want to wrap himself around this woman, and never let go.

Their cocoon of comfort was shattered as she yanked her body away from his, crossing her arms, consternation written all over her face. At a loss for what to do, he shoved his hands in his pockets. Aiden dimly registered the sounds of car engines starting as the mourners lined up to leave, and the whispers of those few who remained.

"Are you coming to the wake?" Her eyes were almost pleading.

"Yes," his mouth spoke without connecting to his brain. His intention had been to pay his respects and leave, unsure if he'd even be welcome. Actually, he was certain he was unwelcome. Why was she asking him, a stranger?

Her head jerked in approval, before she again burrowed in the envelope of her friend's arms, the women then marched away. Aiden hadn't even noticed the blond move toward them. He'd been blissfully oblivious, completely absorbed by a woman for the first time in …forever.

He stood on liquid legs, elbows loose, missing the feel of her. Bewilderment doused his ability to think, as he watched her retreat. Something about the texture of her movement stirred the familiarity again. His memories rose closer to the surface, but faded again as she disappeared out of sight.

The energy in the air was noticeably different. Heaviness descended over him again as he turned to the grave to add a shovelful of dirt. Three other men remained to do the same.

"It's good to see ye again, Aiden. Sorry it couldn't have been under happier circumstances." Harry, his friend's brother, gave him a slap on the shoulder in greeting. The sentiment confused and chipped at his expectation to be treated like a stranger.

He paused to collect his wits, gathering the appropriate words from unused corners of his brain. "I'm crushed that I didn't get to see him again. He was more of a father to me than my own." The truth came rushing out, striking him straight through the heart. "I'm so sorry for your loss." He addressed all three men, again frustrated that he couldn't think of anything better to say. Harry's younger brother, Harvey, and Mr. Saunders, the neighbor from across the street, joined Harry.

Hank had been the oldest brother. A tall and sturdy Irishman with masses of black hair, and a beard to match. The younger brothers had inherited red hair from their mother, but they all had the same goliath stature.

In comical contrast, Mr. Saunders was a petite man with thin white wisps of hair. His eyebrows and eyelashes almost invisible against his pale pink skin.

All three men were in their sixties now. Patches of white had bleached the red hair at the brothers' temples, with several strays flecked about, elsewhere. It was shocking, how much they had aged. He supposed they could say the same about him. He was not yet sixteen when his parents moved him north.

"Would ye like a lift to the wake, then?" Harry asked.

"I don't suppose ye've got a car, at the minute?" Harvey threw a heavy arm around Aiden's shoulder, stretching slightly, as they were the same height.

"That'd be great, thanks."

Harry and Mr. Saunders took a more luxurious, Buick, while Harvey promptly guided Aiden to a rusty, old, Chevy pick-up. He knew that it used to be candy apple red. The painted logo of Harvey's Auto Shop had faded from the hood over time.

The slamming of their doors was loud, but the rumble of the engine was deafening. His shoes slipped and crunched on the collection of empty chip packets and coffee cups strewn on the floor of the passenger side. Harvey looked over to investigate, propping his sunglasses on his nose. "Sorry 'bout the mess. I needed sustenance to get me through the long hospital waits. Just kick it out of the way." He waved his hand as if brushing the offending items away, stirring the smell of sweat and stale coffee.

Aiden took in the scenery as the old truck bumped along; its shock absorbers not up to the task. The town had changed in his absence. Grassy fields had made way for new housing developments. The single traffic light had spawned some friends, though the center of town had mostly remained in its time capsule.

Aiden's knee jiggled against the door as his nervous energy found an outlet. He was still reeling from the weirdest moment of his life. Seeing his friend put underground, and experiencing what felt like salvation all within moments of each other. He had to put *her* out of his mind and focus on Hank.

"How long was he ill?"

"Oh, he had the first stroke about a month ago. It wasn't too bad. He could still talk, though his words were slurred. We thought he'd recover. He was starting rehab, but then he had a massive stroke. Turned him into a vegetable. No coming back from that. He was in a coma for a week before he died. Nasty business, seeing a strong, proud man brought to his knees. Even more horrible, seeing a brother suffer."

Aiden kept a steady eye on the road, using the horizon to ground him, and stop the flow of tears that threatened. He swallowed against a tight throat before attempting to speak. "I didn't know." He cursed under his breath. "I would have come." *I should have been here*.

"I just happened to look up the local paper online. I don't even know what made me do it. His name caught my eye while I was skimming." Aiden swallowed again, and turned to the window to squeeze his eyes shut.

He felt a firm grip on his shoulder. "Per'aps you wanted news of a certain young lady, as well as her pa?"

Hank's daughter, Angel. If he weren't in the habit of denying his true desires, he'd admit that he'd been searching the group of mourners for her. The girl he would never forget no matter how hard he tried. Angel. An appropriate name for the girl who weaved through his thoughts whenever he let them drift.

He sucked in a breath. Light dawned, and memories of green eyes that used to be shadowed behind glasses rose abruptly into transparency. Climbing trees and fishing, later became holding hands and kissing.

Angel.

His plans just changed.

Acknowledgements

I'm going to start by saying how incredibly blessed I feel at being able to share my stories with the world, and to have the support of all the people who help make this happen.

This novella was originally written for the New Love anthology to benefit the March of Dimes Foundation. As soon as I heard about it, I knew I had to be a part of it. I want to thank all the people who bought the anthology and helped make a difference in so many lives.

Sincere thanks need to go to Nicole Moore and the Love Kissed family for their vision and all the hard work they put into making things like this happen. It's mind blowing what the team manages to achieve.

My editor, Eeva, I thank you again for sneaking this one into your schedule. I'm glad you hated the ending, that means it was perfect. ; P

Lorna Bishop and Emma Dixon, beta readers extraordinaire ... you ladies rock. I can't thank you enough for your insight, and for taking the time to read the horrible unedited version! You know I hate commas.

To my wonderful group of friends ... apologies. Again. You know I have hermit tendencies. I live in my head half the time, and I want to thank you for coaxing me back among the living, breathing, real people. You are all so important to me, I don't know what I'd do without you. Lots of love comin' atcha.

My house full of boisterous boys ... You're my little miracles. I didn't know if I could have you at all, and yet here you are. I love your quirky senses of humor and your never-ending energy. You have presented me with my biggest challenge and my greatest reward, all in one crazy ADHD/ ASD/ Syndrome bundle. I wouldn't change a thing. I love you to bits. Thank you, my family, for all your love and support.

I've met some wonderful readers and writers online and in person over the last couple of years. The book community is a fantastic bunch of people and I'm proud to be a part of it. Sincere thanks to all the bloggers who are such a huge part of this group and work so tirelessly with little reward. Thank you all for being awesome. I hope to meet you in person in the years to come.

To all the readers who've taken the time to escape into my stories, a massive, ginormous thank you. You are the reason I hit publish and don't let the pages collect dust in a drawer. It's all for you, guys! I wholeheartedly hope you have enjoyed Angel and Aiden's beginning, and that you will continue reading their next chapter.

Cheers!

Jen x

About the Author

Former nurse, reluctant romantic, and chocolate lover, J.M. Adele, is the author of paranormal and contemporary romance, and romantic suspense. After years of indulging in her addiction to reading, her own characters started to tell their stories. They were relentless, forcing her to put pen to paper and release them into the world.

On most days, you can find her juggling authorhood with motherhood while carrying a book in one hand. When everyone else drifts off to dreamland, she escapes into the worlds conjured by the characters in her head.

Follow J. M.

Links to my newsletter and my Facebook reader group
can be found on my website.

www.jmadele.com

www.facebook.com/authorjmadele

@JMAdeleBooks

@j.m.adele

www.ingramcontent.com/pod-product-compliance
Lightning Source LLC
Chambersburg PA
CBHW020622120726
47905CB00003B/907